Wheelchair Track Events

by Stan Labanowich

Content Consultant:

Scot Hollonbech

Member of Wheelchair Sports, USA

Two-time gold medal winner, Paralympic Games

RiverFront Books

An Imprint of Franklin Watts
A Division of Grolier Publishing
New York   London   Hong Kong   Sydney
Danbury, Connecticut

RiverFront Books
http://publishing.grolier.com
Copyright © 1998 by Capstone Press. All rights reserved.
Published simultaneously in Canada.
Printed in the United States of America.

Library of Congress Cataloging-in-Publication Data

Labanowich, Stan.
  Wheelchair track events / by Stan Labanowich.
      p. cm. -- (Wheelchair sports)
  Includes bibliographical references (p. 45) and index.
  Summary: Introduces wheelchair track events, relates the history of
these activities for the physically handicapped, and discusses
the rules, equipment, and training needed to participate safely.
  ISBN 1-56065-616-6
  1. Wheelchair track-athletics--Juvenile literature.
  [1. Wheelchair track and field. 2. Sports for the physically
handicapped. 3. Physically handicapped.] I. Title. II. Series.
GV1060.93.L33 1998
796.42--dc21   97-19255
                                                          CIP
                                                            AC

Editorial Credits
Editor, Greg Linder; cover design and logo, Timothy Halldin; photo
    research, Michelle L. Norstad
Photo Credits
Betty Crowell, 17
International Stock/Ryan Williams, 12, 33
Tom Pantages, 22
W. Keith McMakin, 6
Sports N' Spokes/Paralyzed Veterans of America, cover, 4, 26,
    28;*Paraplegia News,* 8; Curt Beamer, 11, 18, 25, 30, 34, 36, 40-41;
    Delfina Colby, 14
Unicorn Stock/Mike Morris, 43
Special thanks to *Sports 'N Spokes*/Paralyzed Veterans of America and
Wheelchair Sports, USA, for their assistance.

Table of Contents

Chapter 1
Wheelchair Track

Wheelchair track events are races held on tracks built just for racing. Most tracks are oval in shape. The races cover many different distances. Races have ranged from 36 meters (40 yards) to 1.6 kilometers (one mile). Track races are usually measured in meters rather than yards.

People with disabilities enter wheelchair track races. A person with disabilities is someone with a permanent illness, injury, or birth defect. A permanent disability is a disability that cannot be fixed or cured. Many wheelchair track racers are adults. Other racers are as young as

Wheelchair track events happen on tracks built just for racing.

A camera takes a picture of every racer who crosses the finish l

four or five years old. Young racers are also called junior athletes.

Most racers are paraplegics. A paraplegic is someone who has little or no ability to move the lower part of the body. A paraplegic's upper body is often quite strong. Wheelchair track racers use their upper body muscles to race their chairs around the track.

Track events are part of official track and field meets. Track and field meets include track races and field events. Field events are throwing contests. Some track and field meets include both wheelchair athletes and able-bodied athletes. An athlete is a person trained in a sport or a game.

The winner of a wheelchair track race is the athlete who finishes in the shortest amount of time. A camera takes a picture of every wheelchair racer who crosses the finish line. A timer tells each racer how long it took to finish the race. The best wheelchair track racers reach speeds of 25 miles (40 kilometers) per hour during a race.

Chapter 2
History

Wheelchair track began in the United States during the late 1950s. The first National Wheelchair Games happened on Long Island, New York, in June of 1957. Wheelchair athletes from the United States competed in table tennis, darts, and the basketball free throw. Some athletes took part in 54-meter (60-yard) wheelchair races.

All of the athletes were men. Most had played on wheelchair basketball teams in New York or New Jersey. But the athletes had never raced each other off of the basketball court.

Wheelchair track began in the United States during the late 1950s.

National Wheelchair Games

The National Wheelchair Games have been played every year since 1957. Athletes now train all year long to compete in these games. The National Wheelchair Athletic Association (NWAA) organizes the games and makes the rules.

In 1958, the NWAA added a 91-meter (100-yard) race to the games. Three years later, women started competing in wheelchair track events. The women raced in a 54-meter (60-yard) race.

Wheelchair athletes in the United States raced on straight racing tracks until 1971. That year, the NWAA introduced a 1.6-kilometer (one-mile) race for men. For the race, officials marked out a rectangular, 400-meter (440-yard) track in a parking lot.

Wheelchair racers officially used an oval track for the first time in 1974. They raced around an oval track at the 18th National Wheelchair Games. Soon, most wheelchair track events featured oval tracks.

Athletes train all year for the National Wheelchair Games.

International Track

Outside of the United States, wheelchair track events were not common until the early 1960s. The first Paralympic Games were held in Rome, Italy, in 1960. Like the Olympic Games, the Paralympics are sports contests for athletes from many countries. However, the athletes who compete at the Paralympic Games are people with disabilities.

The 1960 Paralympic Games did not include track or racing events. Four years later, the second Paralympic Games took place in Tokyo, Japan. This time, the Paralympics included a 100-meter (110-yard) race for men and a 60-meter (66-yard) race for women.

Wheelchair Track Today

Today, wheelchair track is a popular sport around the world. In 1996, 3,500 athletes from 120 countries came to Atlanta, Georgia. They came to compete in the 1996 Paralympic Games. Many of these athletes competed in wheelchair track races.

The athletes at the Paralympic Games are people with disabilities.

Chapter 3

Events and Records

Today, wheelchair track events cover the same distances as races for able-bodied athletes. Shorter races are called dashes. The most common distances for dashes are 100 meters (110 yards), 200 meters (220 yards), and 400 meters (440 yards).

Racing and Pacing

Wheelchair racers who specialize in dashes are sometimes called sprinters. Sprinters race as fast as they can from start to finish.

Sprinters race as fast as they can from start to finish.

15

Middle-distance races most often cover 800 meters (880 yards) or 1,500 meters (about one mile). Long-distance races cover 5,000 meters (about three miles) or 10,000 meters (about six miles). The longest race of all is the marathon. This race covers about 42 kilometers (26 miles, 385 yards). The marathon is sometimes considered a track event even though it is run on a road.

Middle-distance and long-distance racers must learn to pace themselves. Pacing means going at a steady speed through most of a race. A racer who does this often has enough energy to speed up at the finish.

Holding races of different lengths means that all racers can compete. For some, races are serious contests. For others, races are a fun way to exercise.

Relay Races

Some track races are team events. These are called relay races. They usually cover 100 meters (110 yards) or 400 meters (440 yards). They may be run on a straight track.

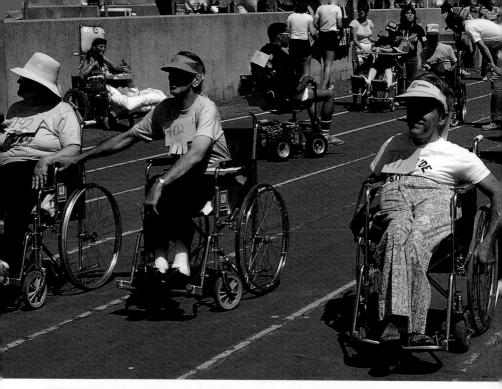

For some, wheelchair track races are a fun way to exercise

Each relay team includes four track athletes. During the relay race, the first athlete from each team races the full distance. The racer tags a waiting teammate, who goes the same distance in the opposite direction. This racer tags the third teammate, and the third teammate tags the fourth racer. The winning team is the one whose fourth racer finishes first.

The Track

Early track records were set on asphalt tracks. Asphalt is a black tar that is mixed with sand and gravel to make paved roads. The first national competitions were held at Bulova Park. The park is located next to the Bulova watch factory in New York. The racers competed on the factory's paved parking lot.

Today, most racing tracks are made of a hardened, rubberized material. The tracks provide a small amount of bounce or spring. This bounce helps runners go faster. But the rubberized tracks actually slow wheelchair racers down a little.

Despite the new tracks, many wheelchair track records have been broken in recent years. This is due to better-trained athletes and lighter, faster wheelchairs.

Record Racing Times

Wheelchair track athletes at the 1957 National Wheelchair Games competed in 54-meter

Many wheelchair track records have been broken in recent years.

Wheelchair Track World Records (1997)

Distance in Meters	Men's Record	Women's Record
100	14.45 seconds	16.7 seconds
200	25.79 seconds	29.03 seconds
400	47.85 seconds	54.62 seconds
800	1 minute, 36.81 seconds	1 minute, 51.82 seconds
1,500	3 minutes, 2 seconds	3 minutes, 30.45 seconds
5,000	10 minutes, 23.66 seconds	12 minutes, 40.71 seconds
10,000	21 minutes, 30.74 seconds	24 minutes, 21.64 seconds
100 relay	53.02 seconds	1 minute, 5.51 seconds
400 relay	3 minutes, 14.45 seconds	4 minutes, 38.23 seconds

(60-yard) races. The winning times ranged from 15 to 17 seconds. In 1961, Ron Stein of the University of Illinois set a record for the 54-meter (60-yard) wheelchair dash. His time of 12.5 seconds was the best in the world. He held the record for several years.

A 91-meter (100-yard) dash was introduced at the games in 1958. The winning time was 27.1 seconds. By 1970, the record time was 19.0 seconds. This record was set by Tom Brown from the University of Illinois. Brown also set a new record for the 54-meter (60-yard) dash. He finished in just 11.9 seconds.

In 1970, Richard Feltes of Illinois won the first 1.6 kilometer (one-mile) wheelchair race ever held. He finished the race in six minutes, 45.7 seconds.

Since 1970, most records have changed many times. An athlete never knows how long a record will stand. Some records last for several years. Others are broken within weeks or months.

Chapter 4
The Athletes

Some people with disabilities are more disabled than others. People whose arms are paralyzed cannot push or race a wheelchair. Paralyzed means unable to move or feel.

Some wheelchair athletes have lost one or both legs due to amputation. Amputation means the removal of an arm or leg. But athletes whose legs are paralyzed or amputated usually have strong upper bodies.

Who Can Enter Races?
A wheelchair track athlete must have

A wheelchair track athlete must have a permanent disability.

a permanent disability in one or both legs. A permanent disability is a disability that cannot be fixed or cured. People with temporary disabilities are not allowed to enter wheelchair track events.

Wheelchair track athletes are divided into four classes. Those in Class T1 are the most severely disabled athletes. They are quadriplegics. A quadriplegic is a person who has limited ability to move the upper and lower parts of the body. Some quadriplegics can push a wheelchair.

Athletes in Class T4 are the least disabled athletes. Most are paraplegics who have some control over their leg and foot muscles.

At a wheelchair track race, athletes compete against others in their class. Men compete against men, and women compete against women. Athletes older than 40 years old also compete against each other. The idea is to make every race as fair as possible.

At a wheelchair track race, athletes compete against others in their class.

The junior division is divided into five age groups. Athletes as young as four or five years old compete against each other. Junior athletes between six and 18 years old can compete in a national championship each year. They compete with athletes in their age group.

Training

Champion wheelchair racers train on and off the track. They try to make their arm and upper body muscles stronger. Stronger muscles help make the athletes faster during races. Many athletes lift weights two or three times a week. They also try to improve their speed and racing technique. Technique is a style or way of doing something.

Coaches help their athletes plan training programs. Before the track season starts, athletes work especially hard to develop strength. During the racing season, they train to improve their racing times. Many athletes specialize in one or two events. An athlete who specializes in the

Many track racers lift weights as part of their training.

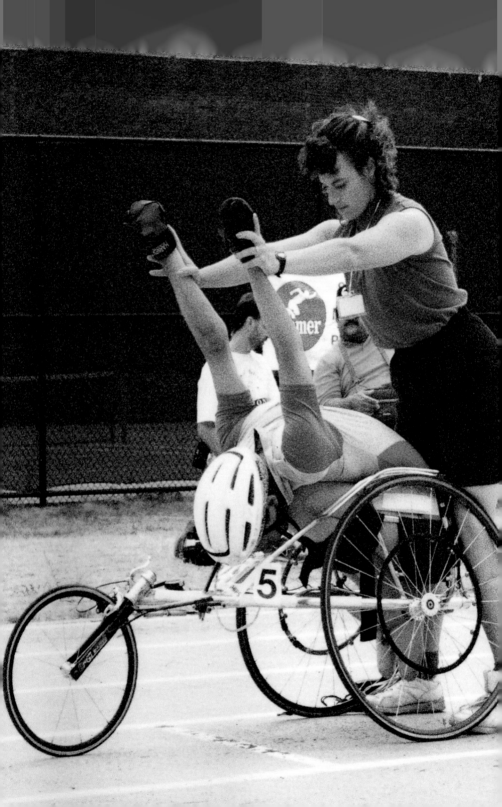

400-meter (440-yard) dash practices racing that distance over and over again. Stretching and light exercise can be part of a training program, too.

The training program of a short-distance racer might include aerobic and anaerobic conditioning. For a track racer, aerobic conditioning means racing long distances at medium speed. Anaerobic conditioning means racing short distances at high speed. A mix of the two strengthens the heart, the lungs, the shoulders, and the arms. Strong athletes are much less likely to get hurt.

Stretching can be part of a training program, too.

Chapter 5
Equipment and Safety

Auto racers want to drive the fastest cars. Wheelchair racers want to use the fastest wheelchairs.

Racing chairs are lighter, faster, and safer than ever before. In the 1970s, a racing chair often weighed 50 pounds (about 22 kilograms). Today, a racing chair weighs as little as 12 pounds (5.5 kilograms).

Racing chairs are made from strong, lightweight metals. These metals were first used to make bicycles. Racing chairs are

Wheelchair racers want to use the fastest chairs.

customized, so they can be expensive. A customized chair is a wheelchair built to fit the size and shape of its user. A wheelchair track athlete may pay $1,500 to $4,000 for a customized racing chair.

Racing chairs are built as narrow as possible. This is done to reduce air resistance. Air resistance is the force of air that pushes against any moving object. Air slows down all moving objects, including wheelchair racers.

A good racing chair should be tight but comfortable. Using a chair that does not fit could slow a racer down. The racer could even get hurt during a race.

Parts of a Racing Chair

Older racing chairs had two small front wheels. Later, the chairs had larger front wheels. Today, most chairs have just one wheel in front. Racing chairs have gone from four wheels to three wheels. The front wheel can be as large as 20 inches (50 centimeters) across.

A racing chair has two bicycle-sized rear wheels. Each wheel is 27 inches (about

Track racers move their chairs by pushing on the pushrims.

69 centimeters) across. The wheels are inflated to help them move quickly around the track. Inflated means filled with air.

Wheelchair track athletes move their chairs by pushing on the pushrims. A pushrim is a metal tube or rim attached to the outside of each rear wheel. It is about one-half inch (1.25 centimeters) wide. It is smaller than the rear wheel.

The best wheelchair athletes travel fast during a race. The racers are often bunched close together. For safety reasons, a bicycle brake is built into each racing chair. The brake is used to stop or slow down the chair's front wheel. Skilled racers avoid crashes by using the brake.

A track athlete steers the chair by turning the front wheel. The athlete turns the wheel with a steering handle. This is a metal bar or lever attached near the front wheel.

The other steering systems found on racing chairs are called compensators. These systems help a racer keep the chair moving in a straight line. Compensators use small, easy to reach handles. A racer can move the handles around with quick hand movements.

Racing chairs usually have side guards and fenders. These are metal shields that cover the wheels. They keep a racer's body and clothing away from the moving wheels.

For safety reasons, a bicycle brake is built into each racing chair.

A small computer is attached to many racing chairs. The computer displays a racer's speed. It shows how much time has passed since the race started. It also shows how much distance the racer has covered. Some computers even measure the rate of a racer's heartbeat. The computer helps the racer keep a safe, steady pace during the race.

Extra Equipment

The athlete's helmet is an important piece of safety equipment. All track racers must wear a helmet for races longer than 800 meters (880 yards). Junior racers must wear a helmet for all events. The helmets are the same kind that bicycle racers wear.

Wheelchair track athletes wear tight-fitting uniforms much like those worn by bicycle racers. The uniforms are made of very thin fabric so the racer can fit easily into the chair. Thin uniforms also reduce air resistance.

A racer's tight-fitting uniform reduces air resistance.

Gloves protect racers against bruises and blisters. Blisters are bubbles of sore skin that fill with liquid. In the past, wheelchair athletes often got blisters from pushing on the pushrims of their chairs. The gloves are made of strong, thin fabric. They protect racers' hands. They also help racers grip the pushrims.

Success

Wheelchair track athletes must be strong, quick, and well-trained. They must use the right equipment and compete safely.

Like other athletes, they know that hard work and a positive attitude are the keys to success. When the race begins, the best wheelchair track athletes are ready to roll.

Hard work and a positive attitude are the keys to success.

sideguard

front wheel

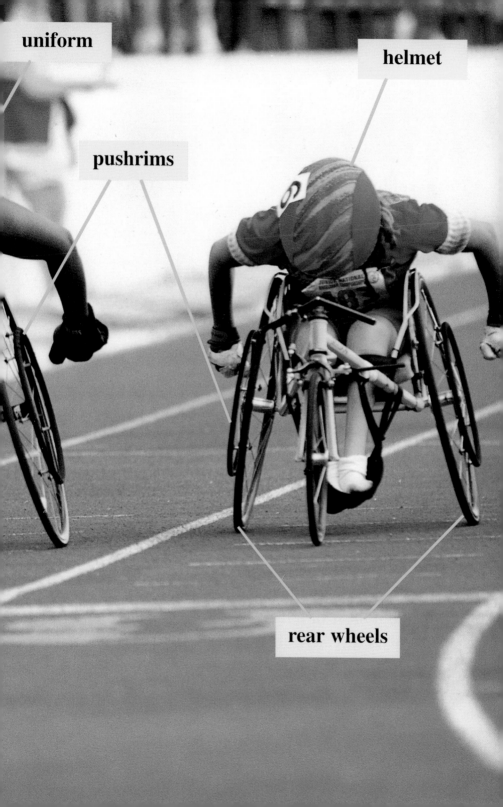

Words to Know

aerobic conditioning (air-OH-bik kuhn-DISH-uhn-ing)—racing long distances at medium speed

air resistance (AIR ri-ZISS-tuhnss)—the force of air that slows down a moving object

amputation (am-pyoo-TAY-shun)—the removal of an arm or leg

anaerobic conditioning (an-uh-ROH-bik kuhn-DISH-uhn-ing)—racing short distances at high speed

asphalt (ASS-fawlt)—a black tar that is mixed with sand and gravel to make paved roads

athlete (ATH-leet)—a person trained in a sport or a game

compensator (KOM-puhn-say-tur)—a steering system on a racing chair

dash (DASH)—a short track race

inflated (in-FLAY-tuhd)—filled with air

pacing (PAYSS-ing)—going at a steady speed through most of a race

paralyzed (PAIR-uh-lized)—unable to move or feel

Paralympic Games (pa-ruh-LIM-pik GAMES)—sports contests for athletes from many countries; the athletes are people with disabilities

paraplegic (pa-ruh-PLEE-jik)—a person who has little or no ability to move the lower part of the body

permanent disability (PUR-muh-nuhnt diss-uh-BIL-uh-tee)—a disability that cannot be fixed or cured

person with disabilities (PUR-suhn WITH diss-uh-BIL-uh-teez)—a person who has a permanent illness, injury, or birth defect

pushrim (PUSH-rim)—a metal tube or rim attached to the outside of a racing chair's rear wheel

quadriplegic (kwahd-ruh-PLEE-jik)—a person who has limited ability to move the upper and lower parts of the body

relay race (REE-lay RAYSS)—a team track event; each team usually has four members

steering handle (STEER-ing HAN-duhl)—a metal bar or lever used to steer a racing chair

technique (tek-NEEK)—a style or way of doing something

To Learn More

Kelly, Jerry D. and Lex Frieden. *Go For It! A Book on Sport and Recreation for Persons with Disabilities.* Orlando, Fla.: Harcourt Brace Jovanovich Publishers, 1985.

Rosenthal, Bert. *Track and Field: How to Play the All-Star Way.* Austin, Tex.: Raintree Steck-Vaughn, 1994.

Savitz, Harriet May. *Wheelchair Champions: A History of Wheelchair Sports.* New York: Thomas Y. Crowell, 1978.

Smale, David. *Track and Field.* Mankato, Minn.: Smart Apple Media, 1995.

You can learn more about wheelchair track by reading *Sports 'N Spokes* magazine.

Useful Addresses

Sports 'N Spokes
2111 East Highland Avenue
Suite 180
Phoenix, AZ 85106-4702

Wheelchair Sports, USA
3595 East Fountain Boulevard
Suite L-1
Colorado Springs, CO 80910

Paralyzed Veterans of America
801 18th St. NW
Washington, DC 20006

Internet Sites

Canadian Wheelchair Sports Association
http://indie.ca:80/cwsa/history.html

University of Illinois Wheelchair Sports
http://www.als.uiuc.edu/dres/wc-sports

Sydney 2000 Paralympic Games
http://www.sydney.olympic.org/facts/paralym.htm

Disabled Sports USA
http://www.dsusa.org/~dsusa

Index